W.S. Thomson & Co.

The First and second Empire of Crinoline

W.S. Thomson & Co.

The First and second Empire of Crinoline

ISBN/EAN: 9783337361235

Printed in Europe, USA, Canada, Australia, Japan

Cover: Foto ©Andreas Hilbeck / pixelio.de

More available books at **www.hansebooks.com**

T is both curious and interesting to trace, from the very earliest ages of the world's history, the ebbing and flowing of that which it is conventional to call Fashion; and however strange and incredible it may at the first glance appear, we shall find, on investigation, that scarcely a single adjunct to the fashionable and elegant toilette of the present day was unknown to races now buried in remote antiquity. From the ruins of Thebes we have a wig of extraordinary excellence of workmanship and finish, mittens for the hands, rings for the ears and fingers, bracelets, pins, bodkins, and brooches; whilst from the excavations of the city of Polenqui, whose history and cause of decay lay hidden in the mists of antiquity, so remote, that even tradition, that many-tongued chronicler of past events, fails us utterly and takes no note of it, we have a female figure with the waist reduced to very slender proportions by the aid of a most complex and powerful system of bandaging.

The early navigators, too, on visiting the island Otahite, or Tahiti, in the then little-known Southern Seas, found the native belles wearing, as an important part of their costume for state and other grand occasions, veritable hooped petticoats, so arranged and adjusted as to show off the waist of the wearer to the best possible advantage. Ornamentation of the most elaborate kind was not wanting to complete this truly primitive but elegant garment. M. Domeny de Rienzi thus writes of one of these Coral Island crinolines, as seen by him gracing the figure of a young native lady who was deputed to carry both presents and compliments to Captain Cook :—" Her robe of light fabric floated over a hamper-shaped frame of willowwork, resembling exactly in form the panniers of our grandmothers."

The accompanying illustration represents the young lady attired for her visit of ceremony to the great seacaptain. Compare the dress worn by these untaught daughters of nature with that of an English lady of fashion of 1713, and it will be seen that the difference between them is extremely trifling, mainly consisting in the presence or absence of shoes and stockings. Compare also the costume of the Otahitan dancing-girl, on p. 3, whose range of experience in matters of dress was confined to her own palm-clad isle, with that of the Venetian lady of fashion of the Elizabethan period, and it will be at once perceived that sumptuous taste and barbaric grace have but an ill-defined line, if any, between them.

The ladies of ancient Egypt, too, had their sashes, waist-belts, and exquisitely fine gauze-like dresses, so fine, indeed, that the contour of the figure could be seen through them ; and it is most noteworthy and remarkable, that although we have no direct evidence of the existence of any contrivance allied to crinoline in its pre-

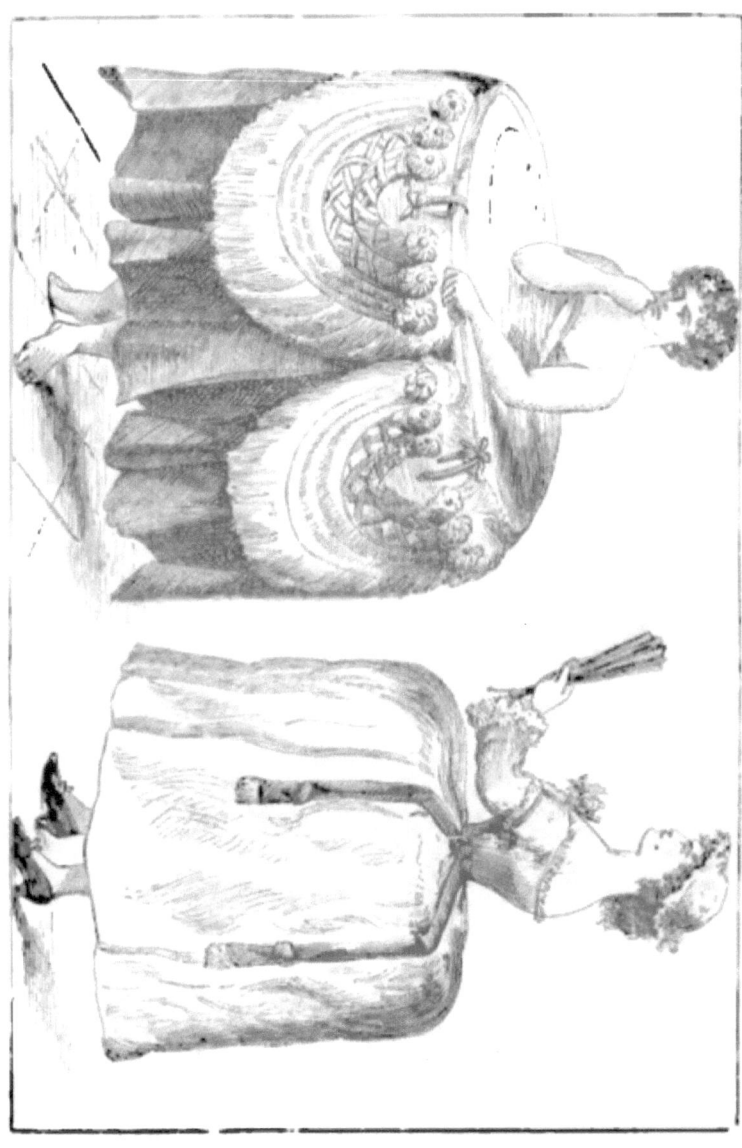

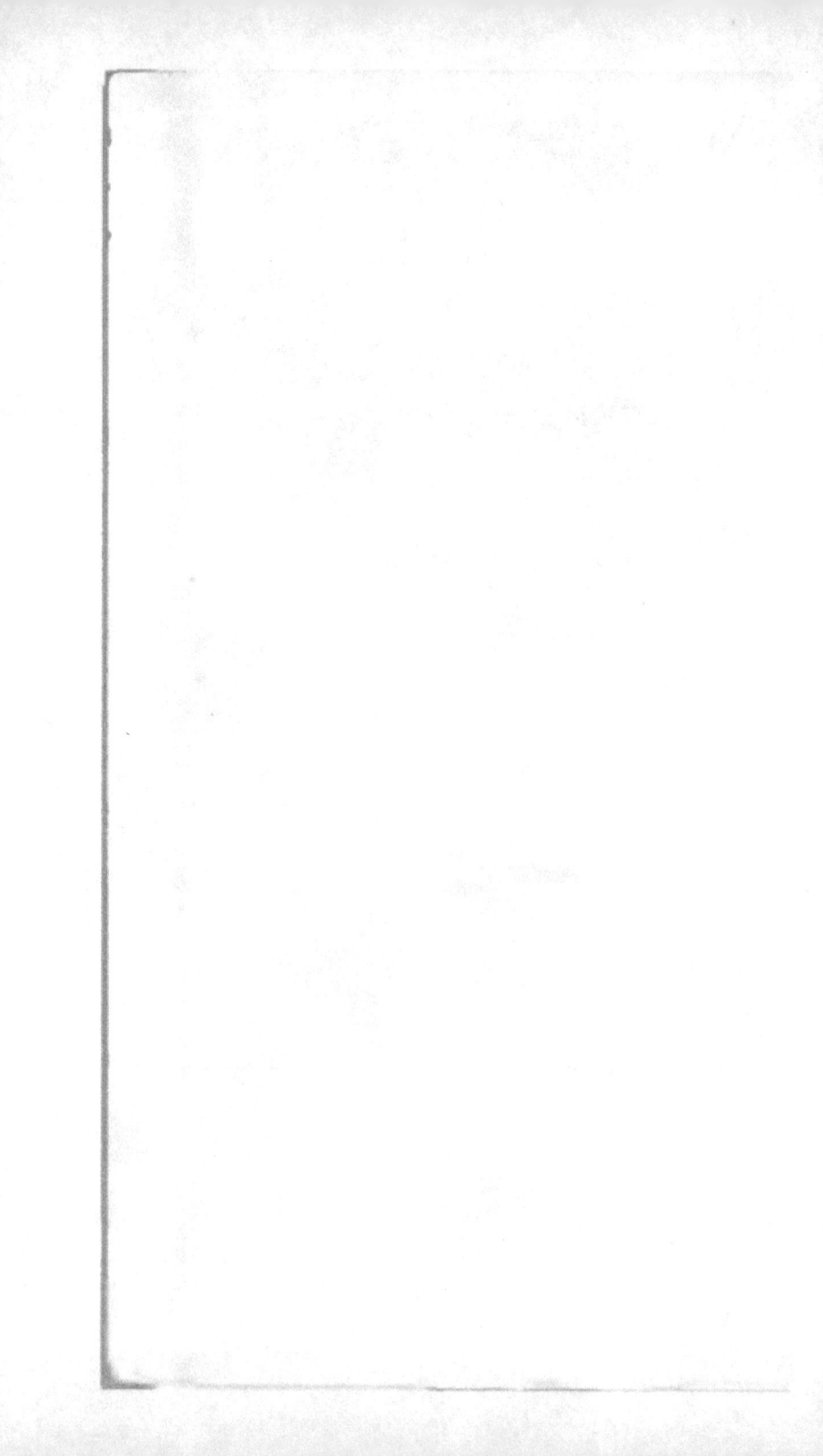

sent form, it is beyond question that the two marked
types of dress—the distended skirt and the so-called
"clock-case" costume—which have, with certain modifi-
cations, had their periodical turn of favour and disuse

OTAHITAN DANCING-GIRL.   VENETIAN LADY OF FASHION.

from the time of the Ptolemies to our own day, were as
well known in the shadow of the Pyramids as they have
from time to time been in the drawing-rooms of London,
Paris, New York, or Vienna.

The accompanying illustrations, sketched from original Egyptian figures, will serve to show the truth of the remarks we have made. The sumptuous raiment and ornaments of the ladies of Israel, curiously enough, differed little in detail from those now in use. We read in the twenty-fourth verse of the third chapter of Isaiah, referring to Divine displeasure manifested against the people of Jerusalem and Judah, and the taking away of matters of personal adornment from the women, that, "instead of a girdle there should be a rent, and instead of well-set hair baldness, and instead of a stomacher a girding of sackcloth, and burning instead of beauty." Further on in history, we find the ladies of old Rome and Greece vieing with each other in the costliness and splendour of their apparel ; and it is most erroneous to suppose, as some writers have done, that the costume of the Roman belles was purely unartificial, unrestrained, flowing, and untrammelled ; it was, in fact, very far from being so. The *strophium*, a contrivance much on the principle of the corset, was used with much strictness in order to form and restrain the waist, round which the richly jewelled band of wrought gold was tightly clasped, allowing the drapery to fall in full plaits and folds over the hips, in such a manner as to contrast with the slender figure above—taperness of waist being as much admired among the ancient Romans as it is in our own day. Terentius, the Roman dramatist, who was born in the year 560, causes one of his characters, in speaking of the object of his affections, to exclaim— " This pretty creature isn't at all like our town ladies, whose mothers saddle their backs and straitlace their

waists to make them well shaped !"   The saddling of the
back here referred to evidently means the application of
some toilet arrangement, by the aid of which additional
fulness was imparted to the robe, with a view to the
improvement of the figure.

The accompanying illustration will not only serve to
show the elegance of the costume of a Roman lady of
fashion of that period, but will also prove to the reader
that the then prevailing tastes and fashions were most
singularly like those of our own day.   The dress of 1790
contrasts curiously with that of old Rome.

It will be needless to dwell here on the various
changes which female, and male attire too, for that
matter, underwent up to the time of Queen Elizabeth of
England and Catherine de Medicis in France. that subject
having been fully treated on in a new work, " CORSETS
AND CRINOLINE." Waists had been reduced and skirts
distended for ages, by dint of one contrivance or another,
until early in the reign of Queen Elizabeth, at which time
Strutt informs us that Scotch farthingales with French falls
were in the highest esteem; his remark plainly proving
that hoops were not only known, but had undergone
improvement before that time; and the illustration on
the next page will serve to show the rather astonishing
costume of the period referred to.   It will be well, therefore, in the absence of any direct evidence on the subject
before Queen Elizabeth's reign, to lay that down as the
period at which the First Empire of Crinoline may be
fairly said to have commenced ; but, as will be seen as
our work proceeds, the clumsy, unwieldy, and cumbrous
farthingales of that period could be no more compared to

the light, elegant, and flexible jupons of our day, than could the huge iron *cressets* of the same date, with their imprisoned mass of smouldering fuel, which only served to make darkness visible, be placed in competition with the electric light. Still, as the sling and the bow gave

LADIES OF FASHION OF THE TIME OF QUEEN ELIZABETH AND LOUIS XIV.

place to the matchlock, that had in turn to succumb to the wheel arquebus,—the flint and steel which followed that, gave place to the percussion cap, and now the cap appears doomed to sink beneath the weight of improved means of ignition, but still designed for the same end,

viz., to *subdue*, to *conquer*,—so with the farthingale.
First hoops of wood, then hoops of cane and whalebone; ever distending, ever spreading, but still ungraceful, unmechanical, and imperfect.

The costume of Queen Elizabeth's reign may be said to
have been mainly made up of stomacher, hoop, and ruff;
and formidable enough they all three unquestionably were.
The ladies of the French court, over which Queen Catherine exercised iron sway at the same period, were not only
laced with extraordinary tightness, but wore hooped petticoats of most voluminous dimensions, in order to give
to the waist the appearance of exceeding slenderness,
in which they succeeded marvellously; and throughout
Elizabeth's reign the hooped petticoat was universal. The
dress of the period was both elaborate and elegant; and
much the same style of figure was maintained up to the
time of Louis XIV., as shown in the annexed illustration.

Bulwer, writing in 1653, thus speaks of the sensation
caused amongst the Turks at their first introduction to
Crinoline :—" I have been told, that when Sir Peter Wych
was Embassadour to the Grand Signeour from King
James, his lady being then with him at Constantinople,
the Sultaness desired one day to see his lady, whom she
had heard much of; whereupon my lady Wych (accom-
panied with her waiting-women, all neatly dressed in their
great verdingales, which was the court fashion then,)
attended her highness. The Sultaness entertained her
respectfully, but withall wondering at her great and spa-
cious hips. She asked her whether all English women
were so made and shaped about those parts; to which
my lady Wych answered, that they were made as other

women were, **withall** showing the fallacy of her apparel **in**
the device **of the verdingale ;** until which demonstration
was made, the Sultaness verily believed it had been her
naturall and real shape."

On King James succeeding Elizabeth, little change
took place in the prevailing fashions either in England
or France ; hoops still remained high favourites, and the
accessories to them were so complex and numerous, that
the toilette of a lady of fashion was an affair of no ordinary importance. Quoting from a play called "*Lingua,*"
written in the year 1607, we find Tactus, the manager, in
sad trouble on the subject. He says :—"'Tis five hours
ago I set a dozen maids to attire a boy like a nice gentlewoman; but there is such doing with their looking-
glasses, pinning, unpinning, **setting, unsetting, formings**
and unformings, painting blue **veins and** bloomy **cheeks;**
such a stir with **sticks and combs, cascanets,** dressings,
furls, falls, **squares, busks, bodice,** scarfs, necklaces, car-
canets, rabatoes, **borders, tires, fans,** palisadoes, puffs,
ruffs, cuffs, **muffs, pufles, sufles,** partlets, frislets, bandlets,
fillets, **croslets, pendulets,** annulets, amulets, bracelets, and
so many **lets, that she's** scarce dressed to the girdle; and
now there **is such** calling for farthingales, kirtles, busk-
points, **shoe-ties, etc., that seven** pedlars' shops, nay, all
Stourbridge fair, **will scarce furnish her.** A ship is sooner
rigged **by far, than a gentlewoman made** ready."

So matters went on, without much change, **until about
the time of Charles I., when** thoughtless gaiety, **profusion,
and fickleness of taste characterised** the time. Marie de
Medici, who, as guardian to the boy-king **Louis XIII.,**
long **led the fashions of the French** nation, wearing **hoops**

of extraordinary dimensions, until, growing stout and portly, distended dresses were discarded, short waists, long trailing skirts, and exceedingly high-heeled shoes became the rage. On Louis XIV. assuming the reins of government in France, fashion received an immense impetus, and the Grand Monarque, together with his gay subjects, dressed in the most costly and fanciful manner, the ladies still adhering to the distended skirt. The fashions thus set in France were not slow in being followed in England, and we find during the reign of Charles much of the same luxury and costliness of dress prevailing. The flowing ringlets, richly-worked lace cuffs, and magnificent embroidery, worn at that time by Charles and his court, were all borrowed from the fashions established by the Grand Monarque.

The Roundheads, under Cromwell, although discountenancing in every way the luxurious costume of their hated enemies, the Cavaliers, still retained the distended hooped petticoat and narrow waist above it. Bulwer, writing in the year 1653, thus speaks of the young ladies of the time :—" They strive all they possibly can, by streight-lacing themselves, to attain unto a wand-like smallness of waist, never thinking themselves fine enough until they can span their waists." That farthingales were in fashion out of England, and were of even greater dimensions than those worn in it, will be proved by the annexed extract from Pepys' Diary, dated May 25, 1662 :— " Looked into many churches, among others, Mr. Baxter's, at Blackfryers. Out with Captain Ferrers to Charing Cross, and there at the Triumph tavern, he showed me some Portugall ladys, which are come to town before the Queene. They are not handsome, and their farthingales a strange dress. Many ladys and persons of quality came to see them."

But never, perhaps, did the hooped skirt arrive at such enormous and formidable dimensions as at this period, reaching its culminating point during the reign of Queen Anne, mainly through the introduction of a new form of hooped petticoat, invented in the year 1709 by one Mrs. Selby, whose new invention appears to have attracted universal attention, for we find a pamphlet written at Bath, and dated 1711, dealing at length with its merits. It is entitled, "The Farthingale Reviewed; or, More Work for the Cooper. A Panegyrick on the late but most Admirable Invention of the Hoop Petticoat." We also read that the widely distended petticoat of this period was sustained on a "*commode bustle*," or dress-supporter, called by the very unmistakeable name of a "*pair of hips.*" In 1710 a certain lady of fashion was robbed by her maid, and the following list of stolen treasures was published: "Four pairs of silk stockings *curiously darned;* three pairs of fashionable eyebrows; two sets of ivory teeth; one pair of box, for common use; and two *pairs of hips*, of the newest fashion."

Remonstrances were earnestly and frequently made, through the medium of the public press, on the alarming subject of petticoats; the thunders of the press, however, utterly failed to bring about the slightest reduction in the size of the ladies' farthingales, but mechanical ingenuity was, to some extent, again brought to bear on them, with a view to imparting a certain amount of portability, and Mrs. Selby stood not alone in the field of improvement. The *Weekly Journal* of January, 1717, announces the death of this celebrated mantua-maker, who invented the hooped petticoat.

Mrs. Stone, writing in the *Chronicles of Fashion,* thus refers to Mrs. Selby :—

"How we yearn to know something more of Mrs. Selby, her personal appearance, her whereabouts, her habits, her thoughts! Can no more be said of her, whose inventive genius influenced the empire for wellnigh a century,—who, by the potency of a rim of whalebone, upheld the universal realm of Fashion against the censures of the press, the admonitions of the pulpit, and the common sense of the whole nation? Mrs. Tempest, the milliner, had her portrait taken by Kent, and painted on the staircase of Kensington Palace; and what was Mrs. Tempest, that her lineaments should be preserved, whilst those of Mrs. Selby, the inventor of the hoop, are suffered to fall into oblivion?"

We find that in 1735 a kind of petticoat, known as the "side hoop," was introduced ; this was so constructed, that by a sort of hinge arrangement it could be folded or doubled on itself, on the wearer entering a carriage or going through a doorway.

Ten years pass away, and hoops are still the rage. In 1745 an indignant author (we presume a crusty old bachelor) wrote a book, which he no doubt considered perfectly tremendous and utterly annihilating to hoops of all descriptions. This triumph of literary skill is entitled, "The Enormous Abomination of the Hoop Petticoat." In dealing with his subject, the author expresses wonder that hoops should remain in favour. He says :—"When the hooped petticoat was introduced in 1709 (referring to the invention of Mrs. Selby), everybody thought it would be out in a twelvemonth at farthest ;" but *as it did not go out,* but rather gained in favour, he proceeds to handle it after his own manner, and classes the ladies who wear it

under five heads or denominations :—" Class 1st, merely
hooped; class 2nd, hooped, and coming into a room;
class 3rd, hooped, and actually in a room; class 4th,
hooped, and in a coach or chair; class 5th, hooped,
and in any public assembly, particularly at church."

In the year 1790 matters remained much as they had
been; seven years, however, brought about strange changes.
The period of the French revolutionary movement and
the reign of the first Napoleon saw crinolines utterly
banished; waists both beginning and ending just below
the arm-pits, coupled with skirts devoid of distension of
any kind, became the rage; and at this point the First
Empire of Crinoline may be said to have ended, and it
was not until the year 1834 that a revival of the old taste
for distended drapery fully established itself, and a variety
of expedients, more or less successful, were had recourse
to for bringing the required fulness about; corded materials, horse-hair cloth, starched muslin skirts, not uncom-
monly eight deep, were not unfrequently employed; and
we know that in America, Manilla cloth was in much
request for petticoat manufacture. Coffee-sacks were at
a premium, being largely monopolised for purposes of
dress-distension; it sometimes happening, that when some
playful zephyr came eddying round a street-corner, and
lifted the charming robe, "Prime Old Java," in letters
large, struck the uninitiated with consternation and amaze-
ment, and led to deep speculation as to why the lady
had thus labelled herself.

As might be readily imagined, matters could not last
very long without change for the better. In 1856
rumours began to be circulated that in Paris hooped

petticoats were being again introduced. The ladies of England received the news with joy. The fashions of good Queen Anne were eagerly consulted; and could the ingenious Mrs. Selby have returned to this earth, her cares would have been in a great degree smoothed at seeing the whalebone and cane ribs, which had cost her so much thought, again, cloth-covered and orbicular, in high favour throughout the length and breadth of the land.

Mrs. Selby's triumph must, however, have been but short-lived, and her eclipsed shade would have faded dimly away, before the bold genius of Mdlle. Milliet, a French lady, who being familiar with the manufacture of watch-springs, turned them to good account. Covering their surfaces neatly with a suitable fabric, she formed circles of increasing amplitude, arranged the series on strong tapes, and so formed the "Jupe-Cage" of France. How the crude and imperfect idea thus conceived was utilised and rapidly improved on by the practical genius of the Messrs. Thomson, of New York; how colossal manufactories of the new Crinolines were established by them in America, England, France, Germany, and Belgium; how Crinolines were turned out of hand by the million; and how this enterprising firm sent the flood of fortune, for which so many wait in vain, in a full springtide to the coffers of Mdlle. Milliet,—have become almost matters of history. Twelve thousand pounds is a goodly sum to realise out of a "*new Crinoline conception,*" and a charming chateau in the south of *la Belle France* is no bad exchange for the shop of a provincial *costumier;* but that sum was paid, and very desirable exchange made, before Thomson & Co. became the exclusive manufacturers, by **right of purchase**, of the *steel-ribbed* and elegant form of **skirt for which they are now so** justly celebrated **throughout the whole civilised world.   Even the** uncivilised **are beginning to appreciate ,the new light ;   the court ladies of Madagascar, on receiving from the Emperor of the French, among other presents, a consignment of Thomson's Crinolines, persisted in wearing them outside the dress, in order that they might not be concealed from the admiring glances of their** friends, and **those luckless fair ones who were doomed to** crinolineless **discontent.**

The short period we have just passed through, in which some vague and ill-defined notion appears to have prevailed among the ladies, that a modification of the dress of ancient Greece might, by the exercise of ingenuity, have the coiffure of China associated with it, has happily and incontestably shown that such an anomalous state of costume was both ungraceful and inconvenient. The reign of Crinoline, if we are not vastly mistaken, is destined to be a very long one, and there are numerous reasons for our arriving at this conclusion. It is a well-established **fact, that the custom of wearing** such an **enormous number of garments as were worn before the introduction of the modern Crinoline, piled one on the other** like **the folds of a fancy pen-wiper, was** injurious **to health on the score of their great weight,** expensive **to obtain and maintain, and was** unsatisfactory in **both adjustment and contour after all.   The modern Crinoline, on the other hand, is light, elegant,** flexible, **cheap, and portable, yielding to every** movement of the wearer, and forming a foundation without which no dress, however costly, can be accurately and becomingly adjusted.

Madame de la Santé, a talented writer on Costume, thus writes concerning Crinoline :—

"The present fashion of Crinoline—a fashion which, having passed through its preliminary stages of exaggeration, is now becoming more moderate, and consequently no longer open to satire and censure—has, I believe, had a large share in bringing about this pleasing result. Everyone must allow that the expanding skirts of a dress springing out immediately below the waist materially assist, by the contrast, in making the waist look small and slender; it is therefore to be hoped, now that Crinoline no longer assumes absurd dimensions, that it will long continue to hold its ground, if only as a protection against the renewal of the old system of tight-lacing."

There are some few amongst us who sneer scornfully at Art, whilst they profess to rapturously admire unsophisticated Nature ; there are others who maintain that such statues as the Venus de Medici are the true types of female elegance of figure. Not long since, a medical gentleman well known in literary circles, who held these views, caused a statue of the Greek Slave to be elaborately dressed in the height of fashion, by one of the most experienced milliners of the West End. The result was, as might have been anticipated, a figure so ungraceful, inelegant, and dowdy, that he at once candidly confessed that his experiment was a failure, and the draped statue a fright. Nature is very beautiful in her own wide domain; but where the elegances of highly civilised and refined society prevail, Art must lend her all-powerful aid, to make Nature even commonly presentable.

The "ZEPHYRINA," an entirely new form of Jupon, just introduced, may be safely laid down as the crowning point of excellence and elegance in this, the Second Empire of Crinoline. Invented by W. S. Thomson & Co., and registered by them, Jan. 16, 1868, no written description can possibly convey a perfect idea of its form, which, as will be seen by reference to the Illustration, is perfectly unique in construction. Complete freedom is given to every motion, in dancing, walking, stepping in or out of a carriage, or even skating; there is no possi-

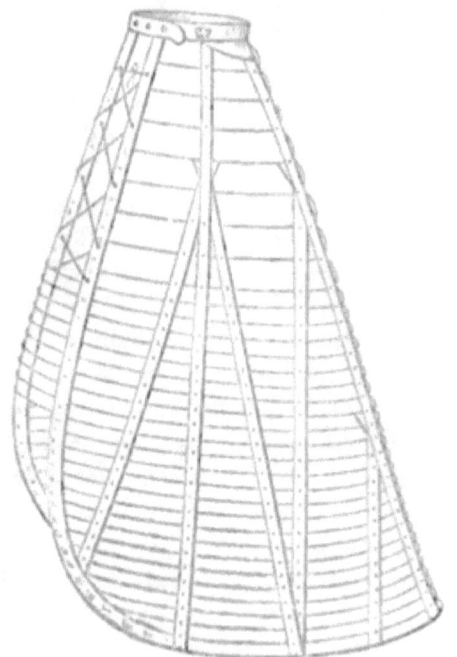

THOMSON'S "ZEPHYRINA" PRIZE-MEDAL.

bility of the feet becoming entangled, and the peculiar form of the front, which admits of regulation at the pleasure of the wearer by means of a lace, insures the perfect set of the garment, over which the skirt of the dress must, as a matter of necessity, dispose itself gracefully. A new and wonderful spiral spring has been specially invented and manufactured by W. S. Thomson & Co. for this, the most perfect of all their inventions.

Manufacturers, dealers, and the public generally, are cautioned against the dangers and impositions of *imitations*.

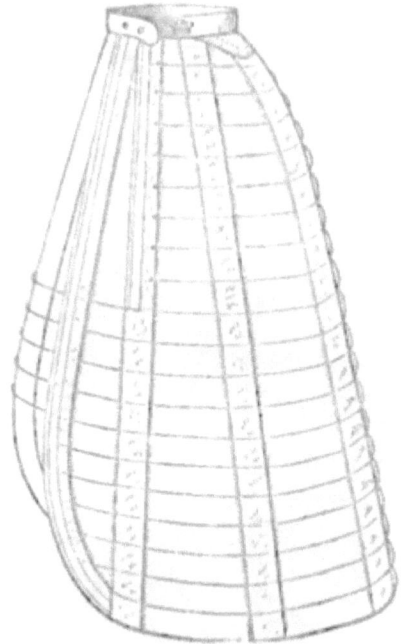

THOMSON'S "ZEPHYRINA" EMPRESS.

The "ZEPHYRINA" for this Season, Spring, 1868, is being made in two forms, which have at once become popular:

"ZEPHYRINA" PRIZE-MEDAL. (Illustrated, p. 16.)

The most perfect *Train* Skirt ever produced; made with Thomson's celebrated Patent Eyelet Fastening, combining lightness with great strength and extreme durability. The only Jupon which will perfectly sustain even the heaviest dress in an elegant train shape. Can be had in white and scarlet. Or partly covered with scarlet or violet French merino, white French Brilliante, or other superior material. Ladies who like *covered* Crinolines should at once see the "ZEPHYRINA" half-lined in this way. (See Illustration below.)

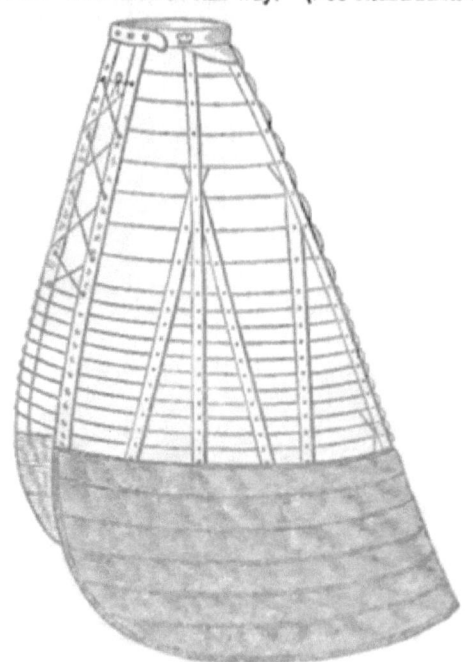

THOMSON'S "ZEPHYRINA" PRIZE-MEDAL PRINCESS.

"Zephyrina" Empress. (Illustrated, p. 17.)

A round Skirt, without train, exceedingly *light*, and especially adapted to the short "costume" dresses now so generally adopted for country, sea-side, and walking wear. (See Frontispiece, which shows the exact effect.) This is less costly than the Train shape, and lighter, being made with beautiful and very broad tapes, woven to receive the springs, which are of the finest, lightest, and most flexible steel, specially tempered by W. S. T. & Co. on their own premises, for this new Jupon. Made in white only, but can be had *half-lined* (see Illustration below) with scarlet, violet, or white material.

THOMSON'S "ZEPHYRINA" EMPRESS PRINCESS.

THOMSON'S "GLOVE-FITTING" CORSET.   Introduced
by Thomson Frères in Paris, 1866, and by W. S. and
C. H. Thomson & Co. in London, 1867.   The most
celebrated authorities of both capitals have published
repeatedly, as their unanimous opinion, " the 'Corset
Gant,' or 'Glove-fitting' Corset, is unquestionably the
very perfection of inventive design and superior manufacture."   Made without gores, in three pieces, cut on a
most correct geometrical principle, by which accurate
fit is perfectly obtained, it possesses the exact same self-
adapting principle hitherto distinguishing the French
woven corset; over which, however, the "Glove-fitting"
possesses the most important advantage, that it will not
stretch in wear.

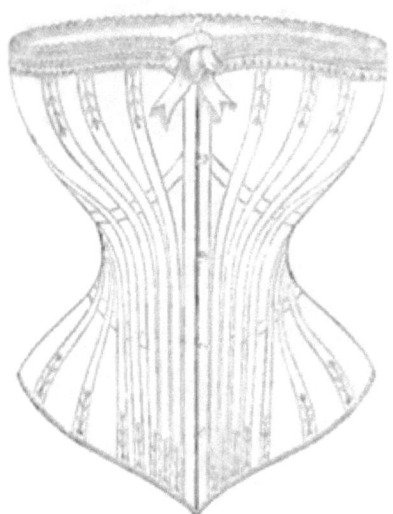

THOMSON'S GLOVE-FITTING CORSET.—QUALITY D.

Ladies are strongly recommended to try, or at least to see and examine, the "Glove-fitting" principle, before buying any other, which may or may not be recommended by a competent and disinterested authority, and to beware of *imitations.* The genuine article is always stamped, " THOMSON'S GLOVE-FITTING," and is made in four qualities, as follows :

THOMSON'S GLOVE-FITTING CORSET.—QUALITY D.
(Illustrated on opposite page.)

The very perfection of make, of the most superior materials, manufactured in a great measure *specially* for this article ; with the patent self-adjusting spring-fastening busk and everlasting silk lace, both manufactured by W. S. Thomson & Co. *on their own premises.* Elaborately boned in a superior and original fashion, with the best Greenland whalebone, every bone stitched through with the strongest and finest silk.

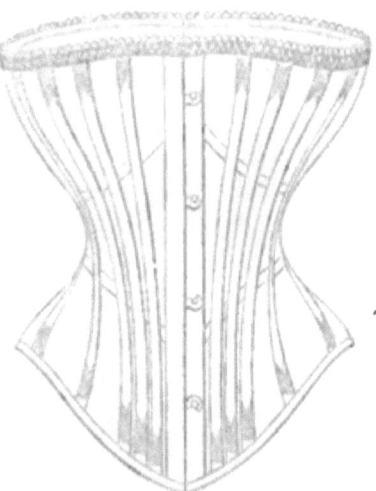

THOMSON'S GLOVE-FITTING CORSET.—QUALITY E.

Ladies who are very particular in the fit of their dresses, and like considerable support without compression, will be charmed with a trial of this quality.

The Glove-fitting Corset, Quality D, is made in white and scarlet.

THOMSON'S GLOVE-FITTING CORSET.—QUALITY E.
(Illustrated, p. 21.)

This admirable Corset is cut and boned with same quality of bone, on exactly the same principle as the D Quality; but being made with fewer bones, is less expensive, for which two reasons many ladies may prefer it. It will be found a most beautiful article at a moderate price, and is made with self-fastening busk and unbreakable linen lace, both manufactured by W. S. Thomson & Co, on their own premises. Can be had in white and scarlet.

THOMSON'S GLOVE-FITTING CORSET.—QUALITY F.
(Illustrated below.)

A most excellent Corset, cut on precisely the same perfect-fitting principle as the higher numbers, made with best Greenland whalebone, but boned in a different and less elaborate form. It is perhaps

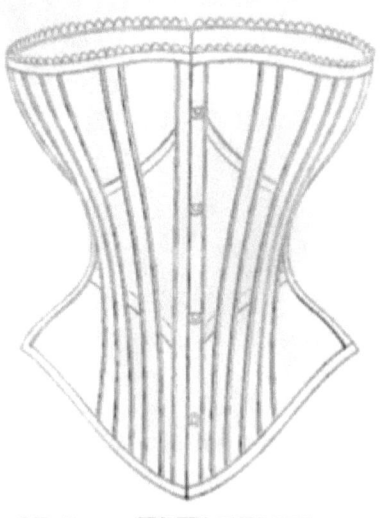

the most comfortable Corset ever worn, and can be sold at quite a moderate price, in white and a beautiful shade of drab dove-colour.

THOMSON'S GLOVE-FITTING CORSET.—QUALITY G.

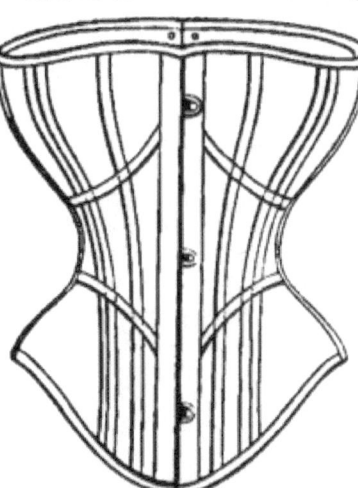

This Quality has only just been introduced, with the object of bringing the many advantages of the Glove-fitting principle within the reach of all. It is cut on the very same model as all the foregoing, boned in the same fashion as the F Quality, but with best French bone, and ordinary busk. Unlike most other low-priced Corsets, it is made and finished with the greatest care, but without ornament of any kind, and will be found the most genuine and economical Corset ever offered to the public at a low price.

The lower hook, which is constructed with a spring, being placed upon its corresponding stud and pressed downwards, the other hooks and studs are adjusted in an instant.

CAUTION.—There are hundreds of imitations of THOMSON'S Manufactures, in both Corsets and Crinolines; but the genuine may always be known by the name "THOMSON," and TRADE MARK

THE MAGIC JUPON.

I SING the Birth of CRINOLINE!—I trace
  From earliest ages its Inception! All
Who wear it, or who swear at it,—attend!
While to the height of this great argument,
Or rather, its circumference, I rise!

When Nature, erst, Primeval Man had formed,
A "beau jeune homme à marier," and *not*
An ape, (distinctly neither Ape nor Monad); he
On this fair earth, companionless,—forlorn,—
To Nature of his loneliness complained.
All-pitying Nature, bountiful and kind,
Bestowed the Woman! Joyful, then, the Man
Courted the Fair Creation to his bower;
But she, all strange and timid, and as yet
Unconscious of her Master,—fled—and dwelt
Apart in shadowy wilderness; till Man—
Poor Man, no whit less lonesome than before,
Again to Nature had recourse for aid;
Nature referred him to her sister, Art;
Art gave the *Petticoat*, a graceful robe,
Flowing and long, with cumbrous folds and full,
And stupid Woman smiled—and—put it on!
Then from her maiden fastnesses was led,
And in Man's house—a helpless prisoner,
Garment-entangled, ever since hath dwelt;
The while her buskined Master, proud and free,
Lord of himself, and lord of his own limbs,
Hath, at his pleasure, hunted, roamed, or fought.

But with advancing ages came the March
Of Intellect—and that of Freedom too.
Began to struggle in the chain each slave,
Each serf—whate'er the colour or the race.
And Woman, too, yearning enfranchisement,
For her long-trammelled feet to win, essayed
The Bloomer! But rebellion so overt
At once was met and crushed by Tyrant Man.

Longer awhile poor Woman stumbled on;
Then, craftier grown, invented *Crinoline*,
Resolved at least, that if, as yet, for her
Freedom was not, her lord should share the chain—
The galling chain—himself had forged for her!
Man, unsuspicious of what lay beneath
The graceful curves submitted to his view,
Nodded approval—lo! the deed is done!
Woman inaugurates the Age of Steel!!

And NOW! proud Man no more with lordly stride
Moves, unimpeded, at his own free will.
Ev'n by his household hearthstone as he sits,
The garments of his womankind impinge,
Banging against his legs! The veriest drudge
Cleansing his doorstep bars his entrance
To his own house! And in the mazy throng,
Where Beauty and where Fashion congregate,
His very form, as Man, is lost,—he moves
Cherubic, nought but head and wings—I mean
Moustache—amidst great clouds of Crinoline!

In vain he calls on all his gods for aid;
In vain he tells Thetimes, or prays Topunch;
Fashion hath said the word, and help is none.
One hope alone remained, one single hope;
Again was Art invoked, and not in vain.
Dwelt in the land a Wizard weird, of power
To make the stiff, the stubborn, flexible;
With magic circles wrought in graceful lines,
He drew down aërial zephyrs to his aid;
Of charmèd steel his mystic spell he wove,
And called it "ZEPHYRINA,"—happy name!
This Magic Jupon NOW the fair encase,
And zephyrs' wings their flowing robes distend;
On watch-spring pinions float their clouds of gauze,
And THOMSON's fame re-echoes through the land—
Dwells in no land a Wizard like to him!